MEET THE GIRL TALK CHARACTERS

Sabrina Wells is petite, with curly auburn hair, sparkling hazel eyes, and a bubbly personality. Sabrina loves magazines, shopping, sleepovers, and most of all, she loves talking to her best friends.

Katie Campbell is a straight-A student and super athlete. With her blond hair, blue eyes, and matching clothes, she's everyone's idea of Little Miss Perfect. But Katie has a few surprises for everyone, including herself!

Randy Zak has just moved to Acorn Falls from New York City, and is she ever cool! With her radical spiked haircut and her hip New York clothes, Randy teaches everyone just how much fun it is to be different.

Allison Cloud is a Native American Indian. Allison's supersmart and really beautiful. But she has one major problem: She's thirteen years old, five foot seven, and still growing!

ODD COUPLE

By L. E. Blair

GIRL TALK® series created by Western Publishing Company, Inc.

Western Publishing Company, Inc., Racine, Wisconsin 53404

 Story concept by Angel Entertainment, Inc. Library of Congress Catalog Card Number: 93-73618   ISBN: 0-307-22007-9

R MCMXCIII

Text by B. B. Calhoun

Chapter One

It is wrong to wear a Walkman in class, and I will not do it again. It is wrong to wear a Walkman in class, and I will not do it again. It is wrong to wear a Walkman in class, and I will not do it again. It is wrong to wear a

Back in my old school in New York, nobody ever got sent to detention. First of all, there were hardly any rules to break. Second of all, our teachers didn't believe in punishment. If you did something wrong, they would send you to the school psychologist. He'd ask you a few questions about how you got into trouble, then he'd write some notes in a notebook and send you back to class.

But here at Bradley Junior High, there are so many rules that no one can possibly remember them all. Sometimes I think that the teachers make up new rules as they go along, just to confuse us and get us into trouble.

It is wrong to wear a Walkman in class, and I will not do it again. It is wrong to wear a Walkman in class, and I will not do it again.

I sighed. I mean, what's so bad about wearing a Walkman to class? It was only math class, anyway. I've always been pretty good at math, but Miss Munson's lecture on complex fractions was totally boring. Besides, it wasn't like I was trying to break the rules or anything. I just wore my Walkman to school so I could listen to this really cool tape that my friend Sheck from New York sent me. The music was so awesome — especially the drum solo — that I forgot I was even in school. I couldn't help it if I suddenly started singing out loud and snapping my fingers. The music was excellent!

I tried to explain to Miss Munson, but she just got all stiff and formal.

"I suggest that you think twice before talking back to me, Miss Zak," she said.

When I told her I wasn't talking back she handed me a yellow detention slip and went back to complex fractions.

I looked out the window at the empty school grounds. Sometimes I wish that my mom and I had stayed in New York after she and my father got divorced. But I guess if we had, I would have never met my three best friends: Allison Cloud, Sabrina Wells, and Katie Campbell.

Which reminded me — I'd better get to work on the two hundred and thirty-one sentences left to do, if I ever wanted to get over to Fitzie's soda shop. Fitzie's is where all the junior high kids hang out. Katie, Al, and Sabs had promised to wait there for me until I got out of detention. I decided to try a new approach. Maybe I could finish faster if I wrote the lines one word at a time. . . .

It is wrong
It is wrong
It is wrong
It is wrong
It is wr-
It is
It is

Just then a paper airplane came flying by

my head. I looked up and saw Andy Grant grinning from his seat in the back of the room. Andy's always in detention and he's a major slob. Just about every day he wears faded jeans, sneakers, a gray sweatshirt with the sleeves cut off, and a red bandanna tied around his head.

Mike Epson was sitting next to Andy. Mike has a spiky blond crew cut and he's about six feet tall. He's been left back at least twice, and spends almost as much time in detention as Andy. But Mike usually gets into trouble without even trying. He's the type of guy who has probably never opened a book. Sometimes I wonder if he even knows the alphabet.

The paper airplane did a loop in the air and landed right on Miss Montgomery's desk. When she saw it, she stood up and curved her skinny lips down into a frown.

"Who threw that?" she demanded, shaking her head angrily, which made her puffy white hair quiver. Miss Montgomery is the oldest, strictest teacher's aide at Bradley. I've heard Sabrina's father tell stories about how she used to run detention when he was in school.

No one said anything. She pushed her glasses up on her nose and looked around the room.

Andy and some of his friends started laughing.

"Now, listen to me," Miss Montgomery said, shaking a bony finger at us, "I want you to settle down this instant and get back to work. Remember, you cannot leave here until you've finished writing your sentences!" She glared at each of us one at a time. "And if I catch any one of you fooling around or talking, you'll get fifty extra sentences to write!"

As she sat back down at her desk, the classroom door opened. I felt sorry for whoever it was because Miss Montgomery gets really upset if you don't come to detention directly after class.

When Mark Wright walked in, my mouth dropped open. I figured that he must have come into the wrong room. Or maybe he was delivering a message to Miss Montgomery. Mark is one of the best students in the whole seventh grade. He gets straight A's in all his classes and never, ever gets in trouble. All the teachers love him. The last place I expected to see him was in detention.

But then I got totally blown away. Mark Wright walked right up to Miss Montgomery's desk and handed her a yellow detention slip! I

5

couldn't believe Mark even knew where detention was. What could a goody-goody like him have possibly done to get sent here?

I looked at him, standing there in front of Miss Montgomery in his green-and-white-striped rugby shirt, white high-top sneakers, and pressed jeans. He was definitely the blond, blue-eyed, all-American, boy-next-door type. I heard that he spent all his spare time practicing the piano. Not cool music like rock or jazz or even classical music, but elevator music — the kind of stuff that old ladies like!

"Well, Mr. Wright," Miss Montgomery asked, "what do you have to say for yourself?" Mark didn't say anything; he just looked down at the floor.

"Aw, poor little boy," Andy Grant called out from the back of the room. "Gonna get in trouble with your mama?" Andy started howling with laughter at his own stupid joke.

Mark straightened up, his fists clenched at his sides, and glared back at Andy. His face was red with anger and his eyes were flashing. "Why, you . . ."

"Andrew! Mark! That will be quite sufficient!" Miss Montgomery snapped. "Andrew,

consider this your last warning. One more out-
burst and it's fifty more sentences." She turned
back to Mark. "As for you, young man, I would
like to see three hundred repetitions of this sentence." She handed him a piece of paper and
directed him to a seat.

Unfortunately, she picked the seat right
behind me. Mark scowled at me and sat down
behind the desk.

"Hey, what did you do?" I asked him.

"Why don't you just mind your own business!" Mark snapped back.

"Well, welcome to the jungle," I said teas-
ingly.

"At least I'm not a savage like the rest of
you," he hissed back.

Miss Montgomery looked up from her desk.
"I don't want to hear any more talking," she
warned.

At that, I started getting angry. I mean, there
was no reason for him to be so nasty. So maybe
I did spend a lot of time in detention at the
beginning of the year — but this was the first
time I've been here in months! So what if Mark
Wright was an A student, a student council
member, and co-captain of the basketball team.

I also know that he's a boring do-gooder, and right now he was turning out to be a real pain in the neck.

"It's better than being a squeaky-clean little know-it-all like you," I shot back, and bent over my paper. It wasn't worth telling him that I haven't been in detention for months, even though he thought I was a regular.

Suddenly, Miss Montgomery stood up. "Whoever is talking had better stop this instant!" she said angrily, moving out from behind her desk and starting to walk down the aisles. *She would make a great drill sergeant*, I thought to myself.

Mark ignored her. "Oh yeah?" he said under his breath. "At least I don't live here!"

I knew I should just keep quiet, but I couldn't do it. Mark Wright wasn't any better than the rest of us — not even Mike and Andy, who really *did* live in detention!

"Listen," I said angrily, "I know you think you're better than the rest of us just because you're supposed to be some kind of model student. But what you really are is a model jerk!"

Mark's blue eyes flashed with anger. His hand was clenched so tightly around his pencil that his knuckles had turned white.

"You don't know the first thing about me, so why don't you just shut up?" he sputtered.

Miss Montgomery marched right up to my desk and pointed her finger at me. "Rowena Zak!" she said. "How many times do I have to tell you to stop talking?"

"My name is Randy," I mumbled. I hate when people call me Rowena, even if that is my name. What could my parents have been thinking of when they named me Rowena?

I looked up at Miss Montgomery. She glared back at me from behind her thick glasses.

"Whatever your name is, you'll be staying here to write an extra fifty sentences!" she announced, turning on her heel and walking back to her desk.

Mark made a funny snorting noise. I then turned around and grinned at him. Miss Montgomery spun back around. "And the same goes for you, Mark Wright," she said. "Just because it's your first time here doesn't mean that you can get away with this kind of behavior." She took a deep breath and shook her head at him. "First, you're caught defacing school property, and now this! And to top it off you are a student council member! I am very disappointed in you, young man — and I'm sure that your parents will be, too."

Suddenly Mark's face went totally white. He turned abruptly in his seat and bent over his desk. He didn't look up again.

Great! Now I had an extra fifty lines to write before I could go to Fitzie's. And Sabs, Katie, and Al were still waiting for me. I was so mad at Mark Wright that I couldn't see straight!

But something else was bothering me, too. Miss Montgomery had said that Mark had defaced school property. That was even against the rules at my old school in New York. It sure didn't sound like something that Mark Wright would do. Maybe this guy had a split personality. I just couldn't figure him out. Not that I wanted to.

Chapter Two

Allison, Sabrina, and Katie were sitting at our usual table at Fitzie's when I walked in. Fitzie's looks really old-fashioned, like it got stuck in a time warp from the 1950s or something. But everybody from Bradley hangs out there after school. I know I always end up having a good time at Fitzie's with my friends.

Sabrina jumped up and started waving as soon as she saw me. If I hadn't been so mad about what had happened in detention, I probably would have played our little game. It's where I pretend I can't see them. It's usually very funny because Fitzie's isn't exactly big. But since I was in such a foul mood, I just stormed right over to the table.

"Hey, Randy!" Sabs greeted me. I threw myself on the bench next to Allison. "What took you so long?"

"Boy, do you look mad," Katie commented,

11

pushing her long blond hair behind her ears. "I can practically see steam coming out of your ears."

Allison looked at me. "What happened in detention? Did you have to stay longer?" she asked.

"I got into trouble with Miss Montgomery and she made me do fifty extra sentences," I told them.

I stole a french fry from Katie's plate and took a sip of Sabs's soda. I almost gagged. I'd forgotten that Sabs always drinks diet soda. Then we all started laughing. It felt good to be out of detention and back with my friends. I ordered an extrathick, double-chocolate milk shake. I really needed it. At this point I really didn't care about the dangers of refined sugar that my mother was always warning me about.

"Ohmygosh! I almost forgot," Sabrina gasped suddenly. She reached across the table and grabbed my arm. "Guess what! I've got the most totally incredible news!" she said.

"Well," Sabs went on, not waiting for any response. "Today I was in the Human Pencil's office, and I heard the most incredible thing."

Katie looked at her. "Sabrina," she asked,

raising her eyebrows, "what were you doing in the Human Pencil's office?" The Human Pencil is what we call the secretary in the main office at school. She's tall and thin, her skin is kind of yellowish, and she always wears a bun on the top of her head that looks like an eraser. Sabrina began to blush. "I was getting a late pass. I know I said that I was going to be on time from now on, but this morning I just couldn't help it." She looked at all of us and grinned.

Then she sighed impatiently. "So, anyway, wait until you hear what happened! The Human Pencil was signing my late pass, and this woman comes walking in. She said that she was Sydney Nelson, the new health teacher."

"So?" Katie asked.

"Yeah, what's the big deal?" I asked.

"Sabrina, we know we're getting a new health teacher," Allison reminded her. "Because Mrs. O'Keefe left to have her baby."

"That's right, and we all know that we have to be in the same health class with Stacy and her clones!" Katie said with a big groan.

Sabrina's eyes opened wide. "I know, I know!" she said impatiently. "But this new teacher is incredible! She used to be a model in New York City and she's beautiful."

"So?" I asked, totally confused.

"Don't you think that's wild?" Sabs went on impatiently. "I think it's so cool. I've never met a real-live model before — except Allison, of course, but she only had one modeling job. Now we're going to have a real-live model for a teacher."

I really couldn't see what the big deal was. New York City is full of models.

"Come on, you guys!" Sabs said loudly. "I bet she'll be fun to have as a teacher."

"You don't know that, Sabs," Katie said logically. Katie is logical about everything.

Sabs shrugged. "Okay, fine," she said. "You don't have to take my word for it. I'm sure you'll just see for yourselves on Monday."

The next day was Saturday. My mom had a lot of errands to do at the Widmere Mall and she offered to drive me and my friends there. It was great. Everybody was free, so we drove by and picked them up. Once we got to the mall, we went clothes shopping while my mother did her errands. Then my mom told us she had a surprise. She bought us lunch at a new health food restaurant called Rapscallions. It was so cool of my mom to take us to lunch. When we finished eating we sat around talking like grown-ups. I could tell that Sabrina, and Katie and Al, had a good time.

On Sunday, we were all supposed to go ice-skating but the weather was bad, so we went to the movies instead. I had completely forgotten about Mark Wright and the new teacher until I was sitting in health class on Monday, waiting for her to show up.

Just after the bell rang, the door opened. We all watched as the new teacher walked over and sat down on top of the desk.

This time, I had to admit that Sabs wasn't too far off. Sydney Nelson was truly beautiful — even for a model. She was very tall, and kind of thin. She was black and had really high cheekbones and short hair. She looked almost exotic, with her huge almond-shaped eyes and big, dangling gold earrings.

The thing I think I liked best about her was her clothing. Finally, there was someone else in Acorn Falls besides me who wore all black. Ms. Nelson was wearing black cowboy boots, black leggings under a black miniskirt, a black mock turtleneck sweater, a black blazer. It was my kind of outfit.

Ms. Nelson definitely didn't look like the Acorn Falls type. Sabs was right. She really did look as if she would be a fun teacher, or at least a little different.

Suddenly I realized that everyone in the room was staring at her, so I opened my notebook. I mean, it's not like I've never seen a model before. I've met a lot of them because my father directs music videos in New York and he's always looking for new faces.

I glanced at Sabrina, but she didn't even notice me. Only Allison was looking like her normal self. She had her notebook open and her pen in her hand and was getting ready to take notes. Al probably figured that this new teacher would be nervous enough with everybody else staring at her.

The new teacher cleared her throat and smiled.

"Hi, everyone," she said. "As you may have figured out, I'm going to be teaching this class for the rest of the year. My name's Sydney Nelson." She paused, smiling, and looked around the classroom. "But I guess you'd better call me Ms. Nelson," she added.

No one said a word. I grinned. I hadn't even thought about a teacher having a first name since I moved to Acorn Falls.

But Ms. Nelson didn't seem to notice the silence at all. "So," she continued, "I hope to learn about all of you as the year goes on, and I'm sure you'd like to know something about me. After all, you all already know each other, and I'm kind of like the new kid here in school."

This was great. Ever since the beginning of the year, I'd felt like the new kid at Bradley. It was nice to think that there was someone who felt even newer than I did.

Ms. Nelson went on. "Well, I'm originally from Minneapolis," she began. "I've lived in New York City for the last seven years, going to school at night and modeling during the day. But now I'm back in Minneapolis. I have a dog, a mutt. His name is Willie, and he's got a black coat and he's about the size of a small pony."

I couldn't believe it; this was unreal — a teacher who actually wanted us to know something about her. Ms. Nelson talked for a few more minutes, telling us about her family and stuff, then looked at her watch.

"I guess we really should get started on some work, now," she said. "The first thing I'd like to talk to you about today is parents." She turned to the blackboard and looked for a piece of chalk. "We're going to make a list of everything we can think of that parents do."

I sighed. This didn't sound like it was going to be very interesting after all. I guess looks can be deceiving. Stacy Hansen, who had been sitting in the front row staring at Ms. Nelson with her chin in her hands, suddenly raised her hand. Besides being the principal's daughter and the most stuck-up person on the face of the planet, Stacy also happens to be a real phony. I could tell she was just dying to make a good impression on the new teacher.

"Yes," said Ms. Nelson, pointing at Stacy with her chalk. "What's your name?"

Stacy batted her eyelashes and sucked in her cheeks. She can be so annoying.

"My name is Stacy Hansen," she said. "I'd like to say that parents provide clothing, food, shelter, and nurturing for their children."

She turned to her friends Eva, Laurel, and

B.Z. with a satisfied smile.

I groaned and looked over at Katie, who rolled her eyes. Leave it to Stacy to come up with an answer like that. She's such a teacher's pet.

"Okay," said Ms. Nelson, writing the words *"clothes," "food," "shelter,"* and *"nurture"* on the board.

She looked at us. "Now I'd like to add one," she said, turning back to the board. "If I remember correctly, parents also do things like make you clean up your room, make your bed, and take out the trash," she said, scribbling with the chalk. She had terrible handwriting.

Everyone laughed — except Stacy. She looked upset and scowled at the whole class.

Sabrina's twin brother, Sam, raised his hand. "I know something that all parents do!" he said loudly. "They have kids!"

Ms. Nelson laughed. Sam is such a clown sometimes. Having kids is definitely something that Sabrina and Sam's parents did — there are five kids in the Wells family. I'm an only child and sometimes I think it would be cool to have a brother or sister.

Then Andy Grant, Mr. Detention, raised his

hand. "Parents yell at you about really stupid stuff, like grades," he said without waiting for Ms. Nelson to call on him.

To my surprise, Ms. Nelson smiled. "That's a good one," she said, turning toward the board. I really thought she was going to give Andy a lecture about the importance of grades or something.

Then Mark Wright raised his hand. I rolled my eyes, just waiting to hear his goody-goody answer. It would probably be worse than Stacy's.

"Parents do whatever they want to and they don't even care what their kids think about it!" Mark blurted out.

That surprised me, too. His answer was not what I had expected from Mr. School Spirit.

Ms. Nelson nodded and added it to the list.

Before I even realized what I was doing, I had raised my hand. It was weird, I almost never volunteered to answer in class. But I liked this teacher. I was definitely more comfortable in this class than I was in any other at Bradley. I could tell that Ms. Nelson really listened to us.

"It's true that parents make lots of decisions

and kids just have to accept them," I said. "Like, if a parent wants to move to a new place, the kids usually have to go, too." I definitely knew about that situation. When my mother decided to move from New York to Acorn Falls, I had to move, too. I probably could have stayed with my father, but I really didn't want to deal with his new girlfriend.

Ms. Nelson smiled and nodded at me and turned to write it on the board.

"Okay," she said, tossing her chalk in the air and catching it. "So basically, parents are one giant pain in a kid's life. They're always yelling at you, or bugging you to do things, or making you go places you don't want to."

Everyone started to laugh. I looked at Allison and noticed that she had stopped taking notes.

Then Ms. Nelson turned serious for a moment.

"Actually," she said. "Being a parent takes a lot of patience, sacrifice, responsibility, and good judgment."

We waited in silence.

Ms. Nelson grinned. "But I don't expect any one of you to believe that for a minute," she said cheerfully. "After all, why should you? And besides, I'm not here to tell you things; I'm here to help you figure things out on your own. And that brings me to our first class project. I think it's time you all became parents!"

Chapter Three

Ms. Nelson stuck her hand into her jacket pocket and took out an egg. Then she held it up for the whole class to see.

"This is our first project," she said.

What did an egg have to do with anything? I was beginning to wonder if this new teacher might actually be nuts.

"First, the class is going to divide up into couples, or families. Each couple will then get an egg. And for the next two weeks, you and your partner will be parents to that egg."

A couple of people started to laugh, but Ms. Nelson put up her hand to silence them.

"Your job will be to take care of your egg as you would your own child," she continued. "And there are a few rules. Since you will be caring for your egg as you would your own children, the egg must never be left alone. Now, that means that each couple will have to share the responsibility for their egg in whatever way they want to. It will be up to you to organize this. And, of course, in order to complete the project successfully, you must make sure that the egg remains safe and unbroken for the full two weeks."

Ms. Nelson reached into her pocket again and pulled out a coin.

"Okay," she said, "*heads* means we put the girls' names on pieces of paper and let each boy pick one or *tails* means we let the girls pick the boys' names."

This whole idea sounded cool. It definitely wasn't the usual Bradley Junior High homework assignment. Actually, it was a lot like something I might have done back at my old school in New York.

Ms. Nelson tossed the coin, and it came down *tails*. So, all of the boys wrote their names on slips of paper, folded them up, and then walked up to the front of the room to put them on Ms. Nelson's desk.

Ms. Nelson mixed up all the pieces of paper, and the girls lined up and got ready to pick out names.

I stepped into line behind Sabrina and

Katie. I wasn't in any rush, but Sabs looked ready to burst. She was so excited.

"Can you believe this?" she whispered. "Each one of us is actually going to get paired up with a guy! And we get to work together with our partner on this project for two whole weeks!" She sighed. "I wonder who I'll get."

Allison was standing right behind me and she raised an eyebrow at Sabrina and laughed. "You know, that's not really the point of the project, Sabrina," she pointed out. Sabrina just gave a little laugh.

Suddenly, Ms. Nelson put up her hand. "Hold on a minute, everybody," she said. "I see that we don't have an even number of boys and girls in the class. There's one extra girl, so would someone be willing to become a single mother? After all, there are a lot of single mothers in the real world. Is anyone willing to find out what it's like to be a single parent?" No one said anything. Sabs looked worried. I knew she was just dying to get a partner. Another couple of seconds passed and I was sure that Ms. Nelson was going to have to pick someone.

Suddenly Allison stepped out of line.

"I'll try it," she said.

Leave it to Al, I thought. She's so self-sufficient about everything that being a single parent might even be easier for her. And she'd probably do the best job of any of us. She's really organized. Sometimes I think she can handle anything.

"Okay, agreed," Ms. Nelson said, smiling. "We'll all be looking forward to hearing about the life of a single parent."

Stacy was the first person to step up to the desk and pick. It figured. She has this way of making sure that she's first in line for everything.

She took her time picking up a slip of paper. She unfolded it slowly, not moving away from the desk.

"Nick Robbins!" she squealed happily.

I rolled my eyes at Katie. It figured that Stacy the Great would get Nick. She's always bragging about how he's her boyfriend, even though we know that secretly, Nick's really interested in Sabrina.

Stacy smiled sweetly before walking back to her desk. "I'm really looking forward to this," she told Ms. Nelson. "Nick and I are very well suited. I just know we'll be the perfect parents."

A few more girls picked names, and then Sabrina was finally at the front of the line. She grabbed a piece of paper, unfolded it, and then turned completely white.

"I can't believe this!" she wailed unhappily, and then threw the piece of paper down on the ground. "I picked my own brother!"

Everybody in the classroom started to laugh.

Sam stood up from his chair.

"Well, howdy, pardner!" he said to his sister in a fake Western accent. Sabs moaned.

I couldn't help laughing, either. Poor Sabs. She's the only one I know who'd have the kind of luck where she'd end up picking her own twin brother. It was really too much.

Katie was laughing too as she stepped up to the desk. She reached down, picked a slip of paper, and opened it. She took one look, swallowed hard, then put a big, fake smile on her face.

"Winslow Barton," she said, trying to sound cheerful. Katie's very polite about stuff like that, but I could tell she wasn't exactly thrilled to be partners with Winslow. A lot of people think he's a nerd because he has a crewcut, thick glasses, and a plastic pocket protector. Actually, he's kind of cool, once you get to know him. I have noticed though that he's not really great with girls. I think he's kind of shy. And he's got some really wild ideas about computers and electronics and things, so sometimes that's all he talks about.

I stepped up to the desk and picked up the the piece of paper closest to me. I really didn't care who my partner was. It was going to be a cool project to work on no matter what. Or, at least, that's what I thought before I looked at the name written on the paper in my hand. "Mark Wright," I said through clenched teeth. I spun around and stalked back to my seat. Now I wished I'd never heard of Ms. Nelson and this dumb egg project. I didn't look at any of my friends. I didn't want any of them to know I was upset about having Mark for a partner.

"I'm going to have the eggs here after school today," Ms. Nelson said when everyone was paired up. "All the parents should come and pick up their egg together. You should then have a planning meeting to decide exactly how you will be sharing this responsibility."

It was hard to concentrate on what Ms.

Nelson was saying. I was too busy thinking about what it would be like being partners with Mark Wright for two weeks. Actually, I already knew. It was going to be torture.

I'm not one to put things off, though. As soon as the bell rang, I headed over to Mark's desk to work out where we were going to meet after school. But he grabbed his books and hurried out the door before I could reach him. I ran after him, but he was nowhere in sight. *He's so weird*, I thought to myself.

Allison walked up behind me.

"Randy, what's wrong?" she asked.

"Nothing," I grumbled.

She didn't say anything else. Al can usually tell when I'm upset about something, and she can also tell when it's a good idea to leave me alone. I'm really glad she's like that. I hate it when someone asks me what's wrong over and over when I don't feel like talking.

Sabrina and Katie joined us and we started walking down the hall.

Sabs turned to me. "You are so lucky, Randy," she said enviously. "Mark Wright is a great guy!"

"Not only that," Katie pointed out, "he gets

good grades, so you'll probably do well on the project."

I was suddenly angry. I had heard enough about Mark Wright, Mr. Model Student.

"Yeah, well, he's not as great as you all think," I blurted out. "It just so happens that it was Mark Wright who got me in trouble in detention on Friday."

They all looked at me, and they were obviously shocked.

"Seriously?" Sabs asked.

"Mark Wright was in detention?" asked Katie. "I just can't believe it!"

I felt ready to explode. Even my own friends were acting like Mark was Joe Junior High or something.

"Believe it! Mark Wright, Mr. Straight himself, was in detention!" I snapped.

I couldn't take it anymore. I spun around and practically flew to my next class.

Chapter Four

"Katie, I have a few things to tell you before we begin," I heard Winslow say later that afternoon as I walked down the hallway with Allison. Winslow was carrying the egg. "As it happens, I have thoroughly researched both the structural makeup and the ideal environmental conditions for an egg, through another science class. During our health class I wrote down all the information you need to know on these index cards." He handed the bewildered Katie a stack of file cards.

"What are you talking about, Winslow?" said Katie, looking down at the cards in her hands. She paused, but Winslow didn't slow down a bit. Just then she saw us and gave us a look of helplessness. I could only shrug my shoulders.

"Katie?" Winslow called out.

After one more glance at us, Katie hurried

along after him. We could hear him starting to explain, "The statistics on the first card reflect exactly how much pressure this egg can withstand from any one point at any one time . . . ."

His voice trailed off as they got farther down the hall. Allison looked at me with one eyebrow arched and we both burst out laughing. Being partners with Winslow was definitely going to be an "educational" experience for Katie.

"What time is it?" I asked Allison for what must have been the tenth time in the last half hour.

"Around three-forty," she told me.

"He'd better show up soon!" I threatened. School had been over for forty minutes. Al and I hadn't picked up our eggs from Ms. Nelson yet and I didn't know when she was leaving. I hadn't seen Mark since class that morning. Just about every other person in the class had already come and gone.

Allison glanced down the hall. "Maybe you shouldn't wait for Mark," she said. "Ms. Nelson might not stay around much longer. We should probably just go and pick up our eggs now."

I scowled. I shouldn't have to go get the egg all by myself. After all, wasn't Mark half responsible for it? If I had known that Mark was going to be my partner, I would have volunteered to be a single mother. Not that I'd want Allison to get stuck working with Mark either.

Allison walked into the classroom. After one last look down the hallway, I followed. Ms. Nelson was reading our health textbook. A bunch of mostly empty egg cartons littered the desk in front of her.

"Hi!" she greeted us cheerfully, looking up from her work. She smiled at Al. "Here's our single mother." Then she looked at me and raised an eyebrow. "Or do we have two of them?"

"No, well, I, uh . . ." I began. For some strange reason I was embarrassed by Mark's absence. "Randy's partner couldn't make it," Al cut in, saving me. "So she's picking up her egg alone."

"Okay, fine," said Ms. Nelson. She gestured at the cartons in front of her. "Take your pick, ladies."

One egg looked pretty much like another to

me. I grabbed the closest one. After Al had chosen her egg carefully, we headed out of the room.

"Congratulations, mothers!" Ms. Nelson called after us. "Good luck."

I looked at Al and then down at my egg. This *was* just an ordinary egg, wasn't it? We walked down the hall toward our lockers. Carrying my egg took up one whole hand, and I had to try to figure out the best way to carry it. I couldn't just sling it over my shoulder and forget about it, like a backpack. And I was afraid to put it in my pocket.

This was going to be more difficult than I had thought. I'd never really thought about how fragile an egg is. I mean, the only time I'd ever thought about eggs was when I wanted an omelet. If I left it alone for a second, somebody might break it. How was I going to manage for two whole weeks? I started to realize that this project would be a lot easier if I had a partner who was willing to cooperate.

We got to our lockers and I shifted my egg to my right hand so I could open my combination lock. I'm left-handed. Suddenly Allison nudged me in the ribs with her elbow. I was so startled, I almost dropped my egg. I was just about to open my mouth to tell her to be more careful when I saw why she'd poked me. Mark Wright was just a few yards away. He was hurrying down the hall with his head lowered, and carrying his books. He looked as if he was on another planet, he was so out of it. He walked right by us and didn't seem to notice that we were there. I couldn't believe it.

"Hey!" I called out to him. "Mark!" But he didn't turn around. He didn't even pause. It was really weird. I looked at Al. She just shrugged.

"MARK!" I yelled in my loudest voice. Luckily, I have a really big mouth, and when I want to, I can be very loud. And, luckily for Mark, he stopped. He was really beginning to try my patience.

"Where were you?" I demanded, marching over to him.

He looked confused for a moment. Then he opened his mouth, looking as if he was about to yell back. Before he could say a word, he noticed the egg in my hand. "Oh, right. Sorry," he said shortly.

"That's all you can say is sorry?" I asked

him, putting my free hand on my hip and trying to restrain myself. Mark was really walking on the edge. "That's just great!" I exclaimed, shaking my head. And he was supposed to be a model student. I looked down at the egg in my hand, and reminded myself that this project was going to be a lot easier if there was a father in my "family." I was actually able to keep my cool and not let loose. I took a deep breath and looked Mark in the eye.

"Okay," I said, trying to remain as calm as possible. "So where do you want to go for our meeting?" He looked at me with a totally blank expression on his face. "What meeting?" he asked. He obviously had no clue what I was talking about.

I sighed, and took another deep breath. I reminded myself that it had to be good for me to hold my temper in for so long. "What do you mean, what meeting? Weren't you listening in class? We're supposed to have a planning meeting to talk about the egg and how we're going to take care of it," I said, keeping my voice as even as possible. I was this close to yelling my head off.

"Look," Mark said, "why don't you just

keep the egg? It's okay with me." He said it as if he was doing me the biggest favor in the world.

"Well, it's not okay with me," I snapped. "You know that's not how we're supposed to do it. We're supposed to share the responsibility. That's why I think we should have a planning meeting right away."

"Fine," he answered, biting off the word. Then he sighed loudly. "We'll have a meeting. But listen, I'm really starved, so could we go to Fitzie's?"

Fitzie's is always crowded and noisy after school. It's not exactly the best place to have a meeting. But I figured I was lucky to get Mark to come to the meeting at all, so if he wanted to go to Fitzie's, I'd go. Besides, If I didn't go now, I would probably never get to meet with him.

"Okay," I told him. "But I have to get my stuff. I'll meet you there in ten minutes."

I turned back to Al, who was still waiting for me by our lockers.

"Here, hold this dumb egg, Al. You know, this is *not* going to be easy," I complained, opening my locker with a loud bang. I tend to slam things around a lot when I'm angry.

Maybe that's why I play the drums.

"I know you'll do a good job," said Al. "Just remember that you're handling something that's very delicate."

"I know, I know," I said, stuffing my books into my backpack with my free hand. This egg was really going to be a problem. It didn't occur to me until much later that the "something delicate" Allison had been talking about might not have been the egg — it could have been Mark.

When I got to Fitzie's, Mark was already eating a double cheeseburger with everything: cole slaw, an order of french fries, and a vanilla shake. He must have been starving! I put the egg down on the table and stared at him in surprise. It was past four o'clock already.

"Won't your parents be mad?" I asked Mark.

"About what?" he asked, his mouth full of fries.

"Well, aren't you going to be too full to eat dinner?"

He shrugged but didn't answer right away. "Not everyone has a guaranteed regular family dinner at night," he finally said.

"Yeah, I know what you mean," I said, nodding and looking at him. *Hey,* I thought to myself, *maybe there was somebody else in Acorn Falls who didn't have a family straight out of* Leave It to Beaver. But I couldn't believe that that "somebody" was Mark Wright. At that moment the waitress came over and I ordered a bacon-cheeseburger, fries, and a soda.

Mark also looked at me with surprise. But I really didn't want to get into my whole family situation with him. My mom and I are pretty casual about meals. She's an artist and sometimes when I get home from school, she's right in the middle of a project and she doesn't want to stop and make dinner. Which is fine with me because then I get to eat what I want when I want.

Anyway, I didn't want to go into all of that with Mark Wright. I mean, it wasn't like we were friends or anything. I didn't even like him. I decided to try to change the subject.

"So," I said, "how do you think we should work this out? About the egg, I mean."

Just then, a bunch of eighth-grade boys walked by our table, pushing each other and laughing loudly. Normally, I wouldn't even have looked up. But this time I had an egg to worry about. I grabbed it to make sure it didn't get knocked off the table. Now I regretted meeting at Fitzie's. It was so crowded! The last thing I needed was to have the egg break on the first day of the project.

"So," I began again, "what do you think we should do?"

Mark studied the remains of his burger as if it were some kind of major scientific experiment. "I really don't care," he finally mumbled.

I couldn't believe what I was hearing. Joe Junior High didn't care? I mean, I wasn't expecting index cards or detailed schedules, but still ...

"Well," I said, determined to try one more time to get through to this guy, "don't you have basketball practice or piano lessons or something on some days?"

Mark shrugged but didn't say anything.

I fought down the urge to scream "Forget it!" and stomp out of Fitzie's. I figured that I had bit my tongue so many times today that it was probably ready to fall off. But for some bizarre reason, this egg was starting to become important to me.

"I really think we need to talk about this," I told Mark. "Otherwise, it just isn't going to work out."

"Listen," he said sharply, "let's just do it this way. You take care of it for as long as you want to, and then you can leave it with me whenever you get sick of having it around." I could tell that Mark was losing his patience.

"Some father you're going to make," I said, half joking. "The poor kid hasn't even been around for a day and you're already deserting it."

"Don't you ever talk about me like that! I'd never be that kind of father!" Mark snapped, his cheeks growing redder and his blue eyes flashing. "I'd never, ever be so selfish that I could desert my kid!"

I was really getting exasperated. This guy's temper just didn't make any sense. And I was getting sick of trying to be so nice to him and having to listen to him yell at me.

"Well," I said, "that's exactly how you're acting right now about the egg. Incredibly selfish!"

His eyes narrowed. "Oh yeah?" he said. "You and your great ideas! You and your precious egg! You don't really care about how anyone else feels!"

That was it. I was furious. How dare he say that I didn't care, when I was the one trying to make the whole thing work out? He was being impossible.

I picked up the egg, and for a second I almost felt like throwing it at him. But that would have ruined the whole project. And Mark was doing a good enough job of trying to ruin it on his own. I didn't feel like giving him any help.

I stood up with the egg in my hand. I could feel my face burning.

"Okay, fine, Mr. Selfish," I said. "Forget it! Forget the whole thing! Forget my ideas, forget the egg, forget we ever had a meeting!"

And before I knew what had happened, I had grabbed my coat and books and was on my way out the door with the egg in my hand.

Chapter Five

"Hey, Sabrina!" called Sam, running through the Wellses' kitchen.

Sabrina looked up.

"Catch!" yelled Sam, tossing something at her.

Katie and I watched as Sabs shrieked, lurched forward, and, after fumbling for a few scary seconds, just managed to catch her egg with both hands.

Her face was bright red. "Sam!" she screamed. "I told you to stop doing that!"

But Sam was already out of the kitchen, and we could hear him laughing as he ran up the stairs.

Sabs turned to us and sighed. "He keeps doing that," she complained. "I'm so afraid that one of these times I'm going to drop it. I can't believe I have to be his partner for another whole week!"

I glanced over to the kitchen counter to make sure my egg was still safe. Sabrina had invited Katie, Allison, and me over for an egg slumber party. After seeing the way Sam was handling their egg, I didn't blame Sabs for wanting to have a few of her friends around. So far, he had hidden it three times and pretended to break it twice.

For me, the week had been much quieter. I only saw Mark Wright during health class, and then we just ignored each other. The egg was fine and I was becoming used to having only one hand. I had to keep it out of my mom's way, though, just in case she decided that it was time to try making egg drop soup or something. She was working so hard on her new art project that she probably wouldn't remember about my school project.

We were sitting around waiting for Al to get there for the sleepover. She was supposed to come over as soon as she had finished eating. Al usually eats at home. I think her mother kind of has a thing about her staying home for dinner.

I had eaten dinner at Sabs's, which was a wild experience as usual. With all the Wells children at the table, along with both parents, it had gotten pretty noisy. And, of course, Mrs. Wells kept piling the food on my plate. She loves to feed people.

Just then, there was a gentle knock on the kitchen door, and Allison stepped in.

"Hi," she said, placing her backpack down on a stool.

Sabs's eyes widened. "Allison!" she yelped. "Where's your egg?"

I looked at Allison, who was empty-handed and still wearing her jacket.

Al smiled. "Don't worry, I've got it with me," she said, unbuttoning her jacket. Underneath, I noticed a little cloth pouch hanging from a ribbon around her neck.

Sabrina's eyes widened. "What's that?" she asked.

"How neat!" exclaimed Katie."It's my papoose," Al explained. "I got the idea from my grandmother. She told me that Native American women used to use a kind of harness to carry their babies."

"Why did they carry their babies like that?" asked Sabs.

"Well," Al explained, "that way they could

keep their hands free to do other things, like gather food. Since I don't have a partner to share the egg with me, this makes it a lot easier for me carry my books and stuff. "

"Come on," said Sabrina, "let's bring our eggs up to my room where they'll be safe."

Sabrina's room is in the attic, so we gathered up our eggs and carried them up the stairs. Then we all stood around Sabrina's room looking for a safe place to put our eggs.

"I know," said Sabrina, brightening. "We can put them in my shoes!"

I stared at her. "I don't know, Sabs," I joked. "You're going to have to walk very lightly."

She laughed. "No, not the shoes on my feet — the shoes in my closet!" she said, running over to her closet and pulling open the door.

We all looked at the shoes lining the bottom of the closet. Sabs has more shoes than anyone I know. She's got all kinds, and in just about every color imaginable. It's like she just can't resist them.

"That seems like a pretty safe place," said Al.

Katie and I agreed, and each of us found a shoe to put our egg in. I chose a dark purple suede flat.

"There!" said Sabs, flopping down on her bed. "My egg should be safe from Sam there." She sighed. "I can't believe my rotten luck. Anyone would have been a better partner than my brother!"

"I don't know about that," said Katie, spreading her sleeping bag out on the rug and sitting on it.

I looked at her, confused. "What do you mean?" I asked. "You've got Winslow. Isn't he the most responsible partner in existence?"

"Sure," said Katie, "but that's just the problem. He's so responsible, he's afraid to let me take care of the egg. Ever! I had to beg him to let me bring it here tonight. He wanted me to call him to let him know I'd gotten here all-right!"

"He sounds like my mother," said Al, smiling.

We all laughed.

"Well, at least your partner wants to help out," I said.

Sabs stared at me. "What do you mean?" she asked. "Isn't Mark a good partner?"

"He's such a good student." said Katie.

"Yeah," I sighed, "but he's being a real pain about this whole project. He's hardly even looked at the egg."

"That doesn't sound like Mark," said Katie.

"Yeah," said Sabs. "And didn't you say he got you in trouble in detention last week?"

"He sure did," I said, nodding. "I know everybody thinks he's some kind of superkid or something, but he's turning out to be one major problem for me!"

Just then the door to Sabrina's room flew open and Sam burst in.

"Hey, Sabrina! Hurry!" he yelled.

Sabs stood up. "What is it?!" she said quickly.

Sam grinned. "CATCH!" he called, tossing a small white object at her.

Once again, Sabs fumbled frantically with the object and just barely managed to catch it. Of course, this time it wasn't an egg but a golf ball. She looked down at it, and then she must have remembered that her egg was safe in the bottom of her closet. Her face turned bright red.

"Just keeping you in practice!" called Sam.

"SAM!" yelled Sabs angrily, raising her arm

to throw the ball back at him. But Sam slammed the door just in time, and the ball hit it with a thud and bounced back onto the carpet.

"That's it!" said Sabrina. "I just have to think of a way to get him back."

"Yeah," I said. "He thinks he's pretty funny."

"I wouldn't want to see him as a father," said Katie.

"He keeps scaring me to death!" said Sabs.

"It's frightening to be responsible for something so delicate," Al agreed. "The other day, I was sitting on the rug in my livingroom, reading, and I had put my egg down right next to me, where I could watch it. I got so into my book that I forgot about the egg. The next thing I knew, Charlie came running through the room, yelling something about Superman or Spiderman, and he almost stepped right on it!"

"I know," I said. "That's how I felt when I took my egg to Fitzie's to try to have my meeting with Mark. It was so crowded, and all these people kept knocking into our table. I guess it's always like that there, but I never noticed it until I brought my egg with me."

A little while later, when we were all lying in our sleeping bags with the lights off, I thought about how I never wanted to take my egg to Fitzie's again, or to anyplace where something bad might happen to it.

Then I started to wonder about my own parents. My mother says that when I was a baby, they took me with them practically everywhere they went. I had never really thought about it before, but I began to wonder how they had handled it.

When we woke up the next morning and looked outside, we saw that it had snowed. It's funny when I first moved to Acorn Falls, I used to get really worked up every time it snowed. But now I'm used to it. It snows a lot more here than it ever did in New York City.

I was just pulling on my favorite pair of black leggings and this awesome black and white oversized sweater that my mom had given me when Sabs let out a little shriek.

We all looked over to where she stood in front of the closet.

"What is it?" I asked.

"What's wrong, Sabrina?" Katie wanted to

know.

"Oh, no," Sabs wailed, looking down at the shoes in her closet. "I put my egg in one of my purple flats, but someone else put their egg in the other flat, and now I can't tell which one is mine!"

"I put mine in a purple flat, too!" I said, hurrying over to the closet.

"I can't remember whether I put mine in the left one or the right one!" wailed Sabs.

"Neither can I," I admitted.

"Hold on," said Katie. "I'm sure we can figure out which is which. I mean, no two eggs can look completely identical, right?"

"But the differences might be much too tiny to notice," Al pointed out.

Sabs lifted the two eggs out of the purple flats and eyed them carefully, as Katie retrieved her egg from one of Sabrina's pink high-tops, and Allison took hers out of a fuzzy teddy-bear-shaped slipper.

"Hmmm," said Sabs. "I'm pretty sure mine was kind of pointy on top."

"Sabs, all eggs are pointy on top," I sighed. "Let me look."

She handed me the eggs. I couldn't explain

it, but it was important to me to get my own egg back.

I looked at the two eggs carefully. I thought I remembered mine having some little bumps on the side, like the one in my left hand. And the one in my right hand did seem especially pointy.

"I think you're right, Sabrina," I said finally. "Yours is a little pointier on top. And I think this one's mine." I handed her her egg.

"You know," said Al thoughtfully, "maybe we should mark the eggs in some way so that doesn't happen again."

"That's an awesome idea!" I said. "We could decorate them. I think I'll paint mine black." I love black.

"Well, I don't think we should go that far," said Katie. "It wouldn't really be fair, not without asking our partners. I mean, Winslow would kill me if I did something that drastic."

"Oh, come on," said Sabs. "I'd love to paint 'Sam Stinks' in giant letters on my egg."

"Sabrina, you can't fit giant letters on that little egg," I said.

"Listen," said Al, "I agree with Katie. We probably shouldn't paint them. The paint would probably strengthen the shells, so it could be like cheating."

"Oh, yeah," said Sabs.

"So what were you thinking?" I asked Al.

"I think it would probably be a good idea if we penciled our initials onto the eggs," she answered. "And you guys should probably put your partners' initials on, too."

"I guess that would only be fair," said Katie.

I knew Al was right, although I wasn't exactly excited about putting my initials and Mark's together anywhere.

After we had initialed our eggs, we got dressed. Then we took the eggs downstairs to the kitchen.

Suddenly Sabrina turned to us. "Guys, look," she said quickly, pointing toward the kitchen window. We looked out and saw Sam shoveling the driveway.

Sabs smiled. "Here's my chance," she said.

"What do you mean?" asked Al.

"To get Sam back!" said Sabs, wiggling her eyebrows up and down.

"I don't get it," said Katie.

I laughed. "Are you kidding?" I asked. "Sam's alone out there in the snow. He's just asking to be bombarded with snowballs."

"Really," said Sabs. "And he definitely deserves it after throwing the egg around this past week."

We quickly put our eggs down on the kitchen counter and threw on our sweaters, scarves, and parkas that hung from the hooks near the back door.

Outside, we hurried quietly through the snow toward Sam, who was shoveling with his back to us. We each scooped up some snow and made a snowball. As I looked at the others, I had to cover my mouth so I wouldn't laugh and give us all away.

"Hey, Sam!" called Sabrina.

Sam stopped shoveling and turned to face us.

"Catch!" yelled Sabs, hurling her snowball at him and letting it land smack in the middle of his chest.

Right away, Sam bent down to scoop up some snow of his own, but Katie, Al, and I threw our snowballs at him, and before he could even finish making his, his wool cap was covered with snow.

"This means war!" he cried, throwing a

huge snowball right at Sabs. The four of us kept making snowballs and throwing them at Sam as fast as we could. We probably would have done okay if it hadn't been for Mark and Luke, Sabrina's brothers. They must have heard us yelling and laughing, because they came flying out the back door to join the fight.

Fifteen minutes later, we were all laughing and covered with snow. Mrs. Wells slid open the window above the kitchen sink. "All right!" she called. "That's enough shoveling for now. Come on inside; breakfast is ready."

We all piled into the kitchen, brushing off the snow as well as we could. I pulled off my big boots and padded into the Wellses' big dining room in my socks. The Wellses are the only family I know in Acorn Falls that eats every single meal in the dining room, even breakfast. I guess it's because their family's too big to fit in the kitchen all at once. "Here you go," said Sabrina's mother, putting down a huge platter in the middle of the table. "Bacon, toast, and scrambled eggs."

Right away, Al, who was sitting next to me, turned to me with a kind of a sick look on her face. I knew just what she was thinking.

"Oh, no!" said Katie quickly.

But Sabrina was already up out of her chair. "Mom! You didn't!" she cried, rushing toward the kitchen.

"Didn't what?" asked Mrs. Wells, as Sam, realizing what was going on, burst into laughter.

Allison cleared her throat. Usually, she's pretty quiet when there are a lot of people around, but I've noticed that you can pretty much count on her to speak up when it's really important.

"Um, Mrs. Wells," she began, "I think Sabrina's worried that you might have used our eggs to make breakfast — I mean, the eggs we're all using for our school project."

Just then, Sabs came back from the kitchen, cradling the four eggs in her arms.

"It's all right," she said with a sigh of relief. "They're safe!"

"Thank goodness," said Katie.

Mrs. Wells shook her head. "Well, of course I didn't use those eggs!" She smiled. "It was easy to tell that someone was saving them for something! They've got a bunch of letters written all over them."

"It's a good thing we labeled them," said Sabrina. "Otherwise, we might have ended up practically being cannibals!"

Sabrina hurried around the table and handed each of us our eggs, then returned to her seat. Mrs. Wells began passing the breakfast platter around, and I watched as each of Sabrina's brothers took a big helping. When it got to me, I took some toast and bacon, but somehow I couldn't serve myself any eggs. I just kept looking down at that little white eggshell with the letters "R.Z. & M.W." written on it, staring up at me from the table.

And when I looked around, I noticed that Sabrina, Katie, and Al hadn't taken any scrambled eggs, either. I could tell from the sort of sick looks on their faces that they felt the same way I did. It was definitely kind of dumb, but I knew that I wouldn't be able to eat eggs without feeling funny for a long time.

Chapter Six

As I slammed my locker shut the following Monday afternoon, Sam Wells walked up to me with his skateboard under his arm.

"Hey, Randy," he said.

"Hey, Sam," I answered. "What's up?"

"Nick, Jason, and I are going skateboarding. Do you want to come?"

I looked down at the egg in my hand. Between all the snow and taking care of the egg, I felt like I hadn't gone skateboarding in a hundred years.

"Are you sure the snow's melted enough?" I asked. "And isn't the ground pretty wet in spots?"

"It doesn't matter," said Sam with a smile.

I looked at him. "What are you talking about?" I asked.

"Luke said he'd drive us over to Wild Wheels!" he announced happily.

"Awesome!" I cried. Wild Wheels was the new indoor skateboard park they'd just built over in Baywood. I was dying to check it out. It was supposed to be totally cool, with a bunch of crazy ramps and stuff. I'd heard that they had this one jump called Devil's Hoop that everybody said was really tough. I really wanted to see if I could handle it.

But there was no way that I could take the egg to Wild Wheels. I mean, I'm really good on a skateboard, but I wasn't about to try Devil's Hoop or any other jump with an egg in my hand. Then I made a decision. I would just go find Mark and tell him it was his turn to take the egg. After all, it was about time he took care of it.

"Sure, I'll come," I told Sam. "But I have to do one thing first."

"Okay," he said. "Luke's got the car in front of school. Meet us out there, and then we can swing by your house and you can pick up your board."

I threw my backpack over my shoulder and hurried down the hall to where Mark's locker was, hoping that I would be able to catch him. I was in luck. He was just shutting it.

I tapped him on the shoulder with my free hand.

"Hey, Mark," I said.

He turned around to look at me. I noticed that his hair was kind of messy. His jeans looked like they needed to be washed and his shirt was wrinkled. He looked tired, too. "Oh, hi," he said.

"Hi," I said. "Um, are you okay? I mean, you look kind of tired."

Mark straightened his shoulders and glared at me. "What do you care?" he asked shortly.

"I was just trying to be friendly." I shrugged. "I mean, we are partners, after all."

"Yeah, well, I'm fine," he snapped. "What do you want?"

"I want you to take the egg for a little while," I told him.

His face darkened. "I can't," he said quickly.

"What do you mean, you can't?" I asked him, putting my free hand on my hip.

"I just can't, that's all," he said. "Not today."

"Hey!" I said angrily. "That's not fair. You said you'd take it anytime I wanted you to. I definitely remember you saying, 'Just leave it with me whenever you get sick of it.' So now

I'm leaving it with you."

"Not today!" he snapped back at me.

I sighed. "What's so important about today?" I demanded. "What do you have to do, practice the piano or something? There's no basketball game, is there? Aren't you going home?"

I noticed his blue eyes grow cloudy. "Yes, I'm going home," he said between clenched teeth, "but I can't take the egg, and I can't tell you why!"

"That's ridiculous!" I told him. "What's the big deal? Why can't you just take it home with you and let it sit there for a few hours?"

"Listen," he said, his face turning red. "Maybe I don't live in the kind of house where you can just leave things lying around like that! Maybe things at my house don't always stay where they belong! And maybe it's none of your business!"

By now, I was so mad I didn't even care what he was talking about.

"Listen, Mark," I yelled at him, "all I can say is it's a good thing we're not really parents. I'd hate to have to spend my life with someone like you! I'd want to split up with you as soon as possible. You know, I'd probably be better off as a single mother, like Allison!"

At this, his face got even redder and he began to shake. He looked like he was about to explode.

"Don't you ever say anything like that to me again!" he said slowly, taking a step toward me, his eyes narrowed, his fists clenched so tightly that his knuckles were white. "You don't know what you're talking about!"

His eyes were blazing as he looked at me one last time before he turned and stormed off down the hall.

I kicked his locker in frustration. I couldn't believe what a pain he was being. Because of him, I couldn't go to Wild Wheels.

I was so mad when I left the building that I marched right by Sam, Jason, and Nick, who were leaning on Luke's car, waiting for me.

Sam flagged me down. "Whoa!" he called. "Where are you going, Randy?"

I turned to face him. "Forget it," I said. "I'm not going with you to Wild Wheels."

"Why not?" asked Nick.

"I couldn't get Mark to take the egg for me," I grumbled.

"So?" said Jason, shrugging. "What's the big deal?"

"Yeah," said Sam. "Just bring it with you. You can put it down somewhere when we get there."

For a minute, I was tempted. Maybe there would be a place for me to put it down, under a bench or something. But suddenly I pictured someone accidentally stepping on it, or rolling over it with a skateboard. I looked at the three of them and shook my head. After the way I had felt with the egg at Fitzie's, I knew there was no way I could take it to a skateboard park. I'd be so worried all the time that I wouldn't have any fun.

"You're kidding!" Jason cried.

Nick's mouth hung open. "You're going to miss out on going to Wild Wheels just because of a dumb old egg?" he said.

"That's right," I told them. "I've managed to take care of this egg so far, and I'm not going to let it break right now. There's less than a week left before the end of the project!"

"Have it your way," said Sam, shrugging, as they climbed into the car.

As I walked away, I could hear Luke start

the engine. I was pretty upset about not being able to go to Wild Wheels with them.

As I walked home, I thought about Mark and his attitude problem. At first I was just really mad. What was his problem? Why couldn't he just cooperate? I mean, maybe he thought I was making too big a deal out of this project, but, in a way, so was he. I mean, I could understand it if he just didn't care at all about the egg, or if he thought the whole thing was a joke, like Sam, but this project actually seemed to make Mark upset. The whole thing seemed really weird to me.

When I got home, my mother was in the studio area of our house. Our house is really great. It used to be a big barn, and everything's really open. There aren't a lot of walls dividing the rooms, so even when I'm watching TV in the livingroom and my mother's doing a painting in her studio, it's like we're still in the same room.

I walked over to see what she was doing. She's been working on these big plaster sculptures lately, which is something new for her. She used to do a lot of paintings, but now she says she wants to break out and try some new stuff, especially since she might have a solo show of her work in the fall at a gallery in Minneapolis.

Right now, she was bent over a big green plastic tub, mixing some plaster into a paste. There was white plaster dust on the floor all around her. I'm glad that my mother can have her own studio to work in here in Acorn Falls. Back in New York, she didn't do a lot of art work. Once in a while she used to do a drawing or a small watercolor painting at the dining room table, but that was about it.

"Hi, M," I said, putting my knapsack down on the floor. Ever since I was a little kid I've called my mother M and my father D. I don't know why I call them that, it's just something I do.

"Hi, Ran," she said, looking up from her tub and brushing a lock of her hair back. "How's it going?"

I noticed that most of her face was smeared with the white plaster powder, and she looked like some kind of wacky baker.

"Okay, I guess," I said, climbing up on a stool and placing the egg carefully on the table that held my mother's sculpting tools. I suddenly thought of Mark and I realized that our house wasn't exactly the kind of place you could leave an egg lying around in, either, and expect it to be safe. Sometimes my mother gets so involved in her work that she doesn't exactly notice things. If I didn't watch out, she might end up mixing my egg into her plaster or something.

My mother looked at me. "Just okay?" she asked, wrinkling her nose.

"Yeah," I said. "It wasn't exactly the greatest day. Listen, M, can I ask you a question?"

She nodded, and went on stirring the plaster mixture in the tub.

"When I was a baby, you and D took me a lot of places with you, right?"

"Sure," she said. "Sometimes we left you with a sitter, but whenever we could, we took you with us."

"Well, what if where you were going wasn't the kind of place you could bring a baby, and you couldn't get anyone to take care of me? What happened then?"

She looked up from her work and shrugged. "Well, then we didn't go," she said simply.

"That's it?" I asked. "You just didn't go?"

She nodded, still stirring the plaster.

"Didn't you feel bad about it?"I continued.

She looked at me. I noticed that a streak of plaster paste had dried on her cheek, and it cracked when she smiled.

"Well, sure," she said, "sometimes I felt bad if I couldn't go somewhere I really wanted to. But when there's someone completely helpless depending on you like that, you don't really have much choice."

I nodded. I thought I knew what she meant. I was starting to realize that being a parent probably meant giving up a lot of things.

"Besides," she said, "we loved you, and that more than made up for any of it."

I grinned. I realized that was probably the biggest difference between taking care of an egg and taking care of a baby. If you loved something, you didn't mind giving up some things for it. And I have to say, it kind of made me feel good to know that my parents hadn't minded giving up some things for me. I looked at my mother, bent over her plaster paste, and I felt a little like I was looking at her as a person, and not just as a mother, for the first time.

"Thanks, M, you're the best," I said, picking

up the egg and heading toward the kitchen to get a snack.

Chapter Seven

The next day when I walked into health class there was a crowd of people standing around Stacy Hansen's desk. Katie had saved a seat for me and I went and sat down, trying to ignore Stacy the Great and her fan club.

"Not only are Nick and I the perfect parents," Stacy was saying, "but we even have the perfect egg. Just watch this."

She put her egg on top of her desk and gave it a spin. It twirled neatly a few times, slowed, and then finally came to a stop. Eva, B.Z., and Laurel, Stacy's friends — and fan club — watched appreciatively.

"Wow!" said B.Z.

"That's really great, Stacy," said Laurel.

"How'd you learn to do that?" asked Eva.

Katie, who was sitting next to me, turned to me and rolled her eyes.

"I guess it figures that Stacy the Great

would have the perfect egg," she said.

"So she can spin her egg," I said. "Big deal. It looks easy." I put my own egg on the desk in front of me and gave it a spin.

But instead of turning evenly, like Stacy's had, it wobbled around until it practically fell off my desk.

"Hey, that's weird," I said, trying again. But the same thing happened.

"Let me try mine," said Katie, giving her egg a twist.

But, like my egg, Katie's barely even turned around. It just wobbled a little and rolled to the side of her desk.

"I don't get it!" I said.

"Don't get what?" asked Al, who had come into the classroom and slipped into the seat behind me.

"Katie and I can't get our eggs to spin," I explained, demonstrating my egg's crazy wobble.

"Of course not," said Al quietly.

"What do you mean?" Katie asked her.

"A raw egg can't spin. The yolk is liquid. If you try to spin the egg, the yolk moves around unevenly, and the egg wobbles," Al explained.

"If you want an egg that spins, you have to hard-boil it."

Right away, I turned to look at Katie. She was staring back at me with her eyes wide open.

"Randy?" she asked me. "Are you thinking what I'm thinking?"

"Well, I'm thinking something; that's for sure," I said, narrowing my eyes.

"What's going on?" asked Al.

"Somebody has an egg that spins," Katie told her.

"Yeah," I said. "And I'll give you one guess who it is!"

But there wasn't even time for Al to guess, because just then Stacy opened her mouth again. "It's easy!" she was saying to Eva. "That is, if you have a perfect egg."

"That creep!" I said, clenching my fists. I could feel the anger welling up inside me.

"How could she?" Katie moaned, picking her egg up off her desk and cradling it in both hands.

"Stacy Hansen," said Allison with a sigh. She wasn't surprised at all. Al had experienced Stacy's sneakiness first hand when the two of them had been picked to model together in the *Belle Magazine* American Beauties Search.

"The only question is, what do we do about it?" asked Katie.

There was no question in my mind what to do about it. Stacy might be willing to do anything at all to impress Ms. Nelson, but hard-boiling an egg was cheating! I'm no tattletale, but I wasn't going to let her get away with this. I stood up.

But before I could take a step, the door to the classroom flew open, and Sabs came rushing in. As usual, she was trying not to be late for class. She had a really frantic look on her face, and she was wearing this new Mexican-style top she had just gotten at Dare, her favorite store. It had big, puffy white sleeves that came down to her wrists. As she hurried by Stacy's desk in the front row, one of Sabrina's big sleeves must have brushed against Stacy's egg, which was still spinning on her desk. The next thing I knew, there was a little "thunk," and the egg was nowhere in sight.

"Hey!" screeched Eva. "Watch where you're going, you klutz!"

"Oh, no! Stacy, your egg!" cried B.Z., standing up from her chair.

"Here, Stacy, I'll help you clean it up," said Laurel, pulling a package of tissues out of her purse.

Stacy's cheeks were pink as she leaped from her chair. "No! No!" she yelled. "Leave it alone! I can clean it up myself; don't anyone come near!"

But it was too late. A few of the kids nearby had already formed a small crowd next to Stacy's desk, and were looking toward the floor, expecting to see a mess.

I didn't waste any time. I dashed over and pushed my way through the crowd. There, on the floor, in front of her desk, was Stacy's egg. It was cracked, but there was definitely no runny raw egg puddle leaking out of it. No question about it. Stacy's egg had been hard-boiled.

"My, my, Stacy," I said, raising my eyebrows and looking down at the floor, "that's a pretty solid egg you've got there!"

I reached down and picked it up. "Easy to clean up, too!" I added, tossing it toward the garbage can in the corner of the room, and making a perfect basket.

Stacy's face was bright red, and you could tell she was trying to think of something to say. Her mouth kept opening and closing, but there were no words coming out.

Nick looked from the floor to Stacy to the floor again, his eyes open wide with astonishment.

"Stacy, what did you do to our egg?" he demanded.

Suddenly the door opened and Ms. Nelson walked in. Everyone was silent. She looked around at the class, most of whom were gathered around Stacy's desk.

"Is something wrong here?" she asked, looking at Stacy, whose face was still bright red.

"No," answered Stacy hotly. "Everything is just fine." She sat back down behind her desk and opened up her notebook, trying to look busy.

"Oh, Stacy's just a little upset, Ms. Nelson," I explained. "You see, she broke her egg somehow." I tried to look sympathetic, but out of the corner of my eye, I saw Katie giggling, and it was all I could do to keep from bursting out laughing myself.

Ms. Nelson turned to Stacy. "Well, that's

part of how we learn," she said, smiling kindly at her scowling face. "I hope you won't feel too bad about it, Stacy. After all, none of us are perfect."

I did my best to hide my face as I went back to my seat. I knew I couldn't look at Sabs, Katie, or Al, or I would really lose it. But as I passed Mark's desk, I couldn't help noticing that he was laughing, too.

Ms. Nelson turned the rest of the class over to a discussion of how we thought the project was going. Stacy didn't say a word. She just kept her face buried in her notebook the whole time.

"So," said Ms. Nelson, looking around the room, "who has something to share with us? Has anyone learned anything new from this project?"

Sabs raised her hand.

"Well, Allison made this really cool pouch for carrying her egg around in," she said.

Ms. Nelson raised her eyebrows. "Is that so, Allison?" she asked. "Do you have it with you? I'd like to see it."

"Uh, no," Al mumbled. I could tell she was kind of embarrassed.

"Well, maybe you could bring it to show us next time," suggested Ms. Nelson.

Al nodded.

"What about the rest of you?" asked Ms. Nelson. "How are the couples working out?"

Mike Epson raised his hand.

"Well," he said, "I'm partners with Michelle Mackintosh, and we figured out this system where she gets the egg for one day, and then I get the egg for one day. It's going pretty well." He looked around, grinning. "Except that I keep forgetting what day it is," he added.

There were a few laughs. I don't think anyone was too surprised to hear that Mike was having trouble keeping the days of the week straight.

A couple more people volunteered, talking about how they had worked out their systems for taking care of the egg. One set of parents carried their egg around in a plastic cup, padded with cotton balls. I thought that was a pretty cool idea. Then there was silence, and Ms. Nelson looked around the room. Then Cheryl Waterman raised her hand.

"My partner is David Kingston," she told us quietly, "and last night he . . . he sat on our egg!" Cheryl wailed. "I didn't mean it," David mumbled, his face bright red. He looked at Cheryl, who was biting her lip and looked ready to start crying. "Honest, it was an accident. I put the egg next to me on the couch while I was watching a movie. I got up during the commercial to get a snack and asked my brother to keep an eye on the egg for a second. When I came back, the movie had started again. But I didn't know my brother had moved the egg! I just sat down and . . ." his voice trailed off.

"Crunch!" somebody called from the back of the room. Everybody but Cheryl and David started to laugh. I could picture the whole thing in my head. David Kingston, one of the biggest guys on the Bradley football team, comes running into the living room with a huge bowl of popcorn in his hand, hops into his seat, and "Crunch!" Slimy, wet, raw egg all over his pants and the couch.

Ms. Nelson raised her hands for quiet, her mouth twitching, her eyes sparkling. "I think we've learned several important lessons here, class. Would anyone like to tell me what they are?"

"Sure!" Sam yelled. "How 'bout 'Look before you sit!'" The whole class broke up about that one, even Cheryl. When we had all recovered, David raised his hand.

"I'll tell you what I learned," he said, earnestly. "First of all, if you absolutely have to leave your child alone, make sure you trust the person you're leaving it with. They should know enough to tell you if anything happened while you were gone. And, no matter what else you're doing, you always have to remember that there's a child around that needs you to protect it."

"Terrific!" Ms. Nelson said, smiling warmly at David. "Anyone else?" she asked. No one raised their hand.

She pointed to me. "Randy, isn't it?" she asked. "Why don't you tell us how it's been going for you and your partner."

I glanced quickly at Mark, but he was writing something in his notebook and didn't even seem to be paying attention. Suddenly I was mad at him all over again. I took a deep breath.

"Well, actually," I said, "it's not really going so well. I mean, my partner is Mark, and he hasn't exactly been helpful. I've ending up taking care of the egg all the time."

Ms. Nelson looked at Mark. For a minute I was really hoping that she was going to tell Mark off. But instead, Ms. Nelson looked back at me and smiled.

"Well," she said, "this is an excellent example of the kind of difficulties that real parents can run into. My advice to you would be to sit down with your partner and talk it out; see if you can reach some sort of solution that's agreeable to you both."

I sighed. I doubted if anything could ever be agreeable to both Mark and me. As far as I was concerned, my partner and I had absolutely nothing in common.

Chapter Eight

For the rest of the week, I didn't do anything but eat, sleep, go to school, play my
drums, and take care of my egg. I was determined to be the best parent in the entire world.
I'd show Mr. Student Council, Mark Wright,
that I definitely did not need him. I only saw
Katie, Sabs, and Al at school. Sabrina was too
worried to leave her egg with Sam for very
long. Winslow absolutely insisted that he and
Katie have a meeting every day after school.
And Allison had to deal with her egg and
baby-sit for her little brother, Charlie, all by
herself.

On Friday, at the end of English class, Ms.
Staats looked at us over the rims of her glasses
and said my three least-favorite words: "Quiz
on Monday."

I sighed. I hated the way the teachers at
Bradley were always giving quizzes. At my old

school in New York, we never had quizzes. We mostly worked on a lot of independent projects, and that's how the teachers were supposed to tell if we were learning anything.

But now that I think of it, a lot of the kids' projects at my old school were really pretty bogus. Like one year in math, all I did was work on this calendar of Women in Mathematics. The class was making it as a project, and I was in charge of the illustrations. It was a lot of fun. I got to draw pictures of all these historic women mathematicians — one for each month of the year — but I practically forgot how to multiply and divide.

Still, I could definitely do without an English quiz on Monday. We were working on boring stuff — diagraming sentences and stuff like that. I have no idea why anyone would ever want to diagram a sentence. It seems totally pointless. I mean, if you look at one sentence long enough, it starts to look like just a bunch of marks on a piece of paper, and it completely loses its meaning. And then what good is it?

No doubt about it, I definitely wasn't cut out for grammar. But then again, I also wasn't doing so well in English, either, and Ms. Staats had really been on my case. I needed to ace this quiz, for sure.

Fortunately, I had Allison. Al's just about the best English student I've ever met. She never has a problem remembering all those weird rules about adverbs and adjectives and prepositions.

As we picked up our books and got ready to leave the classroom, I looked at her, trying to think of how to ask her if she would help me study for the quiz.

"Randy," she said, "Why don't you come over to my house after school today? I thought we could study for the quiz together."

I grinned. I guess I'm really lucky to have Al as a friend.

A little while later, when I was sitting at lunch with Sabs, Katie, and Allison, a strange thing happened. Lunch was meatloaf and mashed potatoes — one of the Bradley cafeteria's worst creations — and none of us was eating very much. Suddenly Sabs stopped swirling her food around on her plate with her fork and looked up.

"Don't look now, Randy," she said, "but

your egg partner just walked in, and he looks like he's on his way over here."

"Mark?" I asked, twisting in my seat.

Sure enough, there he was. At least, I thought it was Mark, but in a way I hardly recognized him, because his face looked totally different. I stared. Mark had been scowling ever since that day in detention. But today he was actually smiling! And he was headed straight for our table!

"Hi, Randy," he called, still smiling.

For once, I was speechless. I did manage to lift my hand and wave it a little.

He walked over to our table, sat down next to me, and took a deep breath.

"Listen," he said, "I just wanted to tell you that I know I haven't exactly been holding up my end of the bargain."

"That's for sure," I muttered.

"I know," he went on, "and that's why I came over. To tell you that, if you want, I'll take the egg for the rest of the time. I know the project's more than half over, but I figure I can at least help out a little."

I shrugged. "Sure, go ahead," I said.

I picked the egg up off my lunch tray and

put it in his hand, trying not to show how surprised I was at the way he was acting. I wasn't about to let him think he was doing some great heroic thing by taking the egg.

"Thanks," he said, looking at me with his blue eyes for a moment before he stood up and walked away.

"What was that all about?" asked Sabs, once he was gone.

"Who knows?" I said. "And who cares, as long as he's finally taking his turn!"

I glanced at Al, but she was concentrating on peeling her orange, and she looked like she hadn't even really noticed what had just happened.

"Come on in," said Al, opening the front door to her house.

We took off our jackets and went straight to the kitchen to get a snack. I'm always totally starving right after school. I don't know what it is, but by the time I get home I usually feel like I could eat everything in sight.

When we got to the kitchen, Al's grandmother was there, standing at the stove and stirring something in a big pot. Al's grandmother is a wonderful cook. I remember when the bus broke down on the class ski trip to Eagle Mountain, and we were all starving. Al pulled out these great-tasting corn cakes that her grandmother had made, and saved the day.

"Hi, Nooma," said Al, putting her backpack down on a kitchen chair and heading for the fridge. Al's whole family calls her grandmother Nooma. Al says it has something to do with the Chippewa name for Grandma.

Al took out a jar of peanut butter from the fridge and a box of crackers from the cabinet. We poured ourselves a couple of glasses of lemonade and decided to eat our snack in Al's room.

When we got there, Al slipped her papoose off her neck and placed her egg gently in a little basket on her dresser. Then the two of us settled down into Allison's window seat to eat our snacks and start studying.

"So, Randy," she said, between bites of peanut butter and crackers, "what do you think made Mark decide to take the egg all of a sudden?"

I looked at her. I should have known better than to think that she hadn't seen what had happened with Mark in the cafeteria. Al may not always have something to say, but she definitely notices things.

I shrugged. "I don't know," I said, spreading some peanutbutter on a cracker and popping it into my mouth. "I gueth he dethided to act like a perthon for a change, inthead of a monthter." I gulped and tried to lick the peanutbutter from the roof of my mouth. "Forget about him, though; let's get started on the grammar."

Al just looked at me for a second, then opened her English book. I couldn't believe that I was the one pushing us to start studying. But I was getting sick of talking about Mark Wright.

"Okay," said Al. "Let's start with prepositional phrases. One of the best ways to figure out which word is a preposition is to put it into a sentence like 'The mouse ran under the piano.' See, words like under, behind, over, through, and around are all prepositions."

After about twenty minutes of studying, we had totally covered prepositional phrases. I felt like I really understood them. I realized that Al's much better at explaining this stuff than

Ms. Staats will ever be.

Suddenly Al closed her book and turned to me.

"You know," she said. "I've been thinking."

I looked up from the book in front of me.

"What about?" I asked.

"About Mark Wright," she said.

"Oh, him." I mumbled.

"Yes. I was thinking that maybe his acting weird has something to do with the fact that his parents are splitting up," she said calmly.

I stared at her. "His parents are what?!" I demanded.

"They're splitting up," Al repeated quietly. "Right now they're in the middle of getting divorced. So I was thinking that perhaps that's the reason he seems so upset lately."

"How do you know his parents are getting a divorce?" I asked her.

"Well, my father mentioned it one night at dinner. Another lawyer in his office is working on their divorce."

I looked at her. "Al, do you mean to tell me that you've known this all along?"

She nodded.

"Well, why didn't you tell me?!" I demanded of Allison.

"I thought it might be private. I mean, I don't really know how it feels to go through something like that. I've never even heard my parents fight. But I noticed that you don't like to talk about your parents' divorce, so I figure Mark feels the same way."

I sighed. "But, Allison, telling me isn't exactly spreading the news all over town," I said. "Didn't you think that maybe it might be good for me to know this, since he's my egg partner?"

She nodded. "Yes, I did, and after I had thought about it for a while, I decided to tell you."

I shook my head. Al always makes sense somehow.

We went back to studying, but it was hard for me to concentrate on direct objects and indirect objects. I was too busy thinking about what Allison had said.

When my parents first told me they were getting a divorce, I got really mad at them. I thought that they were being really selfish, breaking up our family like that. I kept thinking that it wasn't fair, that if they really loved me they would get back together.

I was also pretty scared. I wondered what was going to happen to me. I mean, I loved them both. I didn't want to have to make a choice between them. Sometimes it's still really hard. I miss my dad a lot.

For a while, I stopped hanging around with my friends in New York. I guess I just wanted to be left alone. And then, when M and I moved out here to Acorn Falls, I didn't even try to make friends at first. I just hurt too much. I still don't like to talk about it.

"Randy," Allison said quietly, interrupting my thoughts, "I think maybe it would be better if we got together on Sunday afternoon to finish studying."

I looked at her. "Yeah, I think you're right. I'm just not concentrating."

Allison nodded and helped me gather up my books. I said good-bye and started home, still thinking about the way my parents' divorce had made me feel. Before I knew it, I was thinking about Mark's behavior in a whole new way. Sure, he had been grumpy and even totally nasty, but all of a sudden, it was beginning to make sense to me. I knew that there were times when I had been upset about something to do with my parents, and my behavior had probably seemed totally jerky.

Like the last time I visited my father in New York. I had gotten really fed up with the way my father's girlfriend, Leighton, was always with us whenever we did anything. So I guess I started acting kind of cold to my dad. I even left to come back to Acorn Falls a day early. I never told him why, so I'm sure he was a little confused about the whole thing.

And my parents definitely confused me sometimes. Like, when I found out that my mother wanted to stay in Acorn Falls instead of going back to New York. We had planned to go back to New York at the end of the school year and then she decided that she wanted to stay in Acorn Falls. It was strange to have to make a decision about whether I wanted to stay in Acorn Falls or go back to New York and live with my father. I know I was a real pain in the neck to be around for a few days. On top of that, I took all my anger out on Sabs, Katie, and Al.

When I got home, I had made up my mind

to say something to Mark on Monday. I didn't know what it would be yet, but I just had to talk to him. Maybe he needed to know that somebody understood.

Monday came, and I did pretty well on the quiz, thanks to Al and our Sunday study session. As soon as school let out I packed my books quickly and headed toward Mark's locker. He wasn't there, so I waited for about fifteen minutes, but he still didn't show up.

I knew I couldn't have missed him, since I had reached his locker so quickly. Then I started wondering if he might have had basketball practice or something, but when I checked the gym, it was empty. Maybe he had gotten detention again. I wouldn't have been too surprised, with the way he'd been acting lately.

As I walked toward the detention room, I felt a creepy feeling in my stomach. Who would believe that I would ever go to detention voluntarily?

When I got there, I looked through the little glass window in the door. Miss Montgomery was sitting at her desk in the front, shaking her bony finger in the air and yelling. Right away Andy Grant noticed me looking through the window, stuck out his tongue, and sent a paper airplane in my direction. Mark was nowhere in sight, though, so I hurried off before Miss Montgomery decided to investigate what Andy was making faces at.

Where could Mark be? I was running out of places to look. I tried to remember what else I had done when my parents started to break up. Maybe that would give me some kind of clue to where Mark was. I remembered that I had spent a lot of time playing my drums — really loud — and riding my skateboard all over the place. Suddenly it hit me. Mark played the piano! I headed toward the music rooms. Maybe I would find him there.

As I walked down the hall in that direction, I heard someone playing the piano. I stopped in front of the room that the sound was coming from and pushed open the door.

Sure enough, Mark was inside. He was so busy playing that he didn't even notice me at first. His hands were pounding furiously, and his head was swaying to the music. In front of him on the piano was the egg, leaning against a pile of books. It was kind of funny. It looked like he was giving a concert for the egg.

As I said before, Mark's idea of music is definitely not my idea of music. But there was something about the song Mark was playing that I liked. It reminded me of thunder, or of the way I feel when I'm headed downhill on my skateboard. The music gave me an awesome feeling and I didn't want Mark to stop playing.

When the piece was finished, Mark looked up at me and smiled.

"Hi," he said softly. "I guess you came to check on the egg." He picked it up and held it out toward me. "Here it is, you can check it out yourself. No bruises, bumps, scrapes, or cracks."

I took the egg from him carefully and sat down on one of the folding chairs that the band used for practice. Mark sat back down at the piano and began playing scales up and down the keys. I moved a music stand out of the way so that I could still see him.

"You know," I said, clearing my throat. "There's something I want to tell you."

Mark's fingers stopped playing with the keys, and he looked over at me.

"Well," I went on. "It's just about what I

said about Allison being lucky to be a single mother."

I saw his eyes darken, and I hurried on. "I want you to know that I didn't really mean that," I said. "I mean, I should know. You see, Al's not the only single mother I know."

He looked at me.

"My mom's one, too," I told him.

He wrinkled his forehead. "What do you mean?" he asked.

"Just what I said," I snapped, a little exasperated. For a straight-A student, Mark was turning out to be pretty thick. I stood up and started to walk back and forth in front of Mark. "I live alone with my mother," I explained. "And my father lives in New York City."

His eyes opened wide. "You mean, your parents are divorced?" he asked.

"Sure," I said, shrugging. I didn't mind his knowing about my parents, but I really didn't feel like making a big deal about it.

"But how can you look so calm?" he wanted to know. "I mean, doesn't it just make you feel like you want to explode?"

"It's really not that big a deal," I said. "I mean, in New York, lots of my friends' parents were divorced."

I walked over and carefully put the egg back on the piano. I noticed that he was biting his lower lip.

"But I guess it just doesn't happen that much out here in Acorn Falls," I added. "Not too many kids would understand."

Mark didn't say anything.

As I headed back toward the door, I turned to look at him.

"Listen," I said. "What was that thing you were playing when I first came in?"

He looked up. *"The Jupiter Symphony?"* he asked.

"Whatever it was. I liked it. It was kind of wild-sounding."

Mark nodded and kind of smiled.

"Yeah," he said. "It's by Mozart. He was kind of a wild guy."

"I guess that's why I liked it," I said.

"Yeah," said Mark. "Me, too."

As I pushed open the door and walked back into the hall, I realized that Mark and I might have more in common than I had thought. Then I started to laugh. I wondered if Mozart's parents had been divorced, too.

Chapter Nine

Finally, it was Tuesday, the last day of the two-week egg project.

Ms. Nelson sat on her desk in front of the class. As usual, she was dressed in black. She was wearing a black, brushed cotton jumpsuit and an oversized black jacket with red lining. She had a big red barrette holding her hair back and bright red pumps on her feet. I definitely had to ask her where she shopped.

Sabrina, Katie, Al, and I were sitting together. Mark was a row ahead, with the egg safely on the desk in front of him.

Ms. Nelson looked around the classroom.

"Well," she said. "Here we are, two weeks later. Most of you seem to have survived this experiment." She paused. "And *most* of your eggs have survived."

There were some snickers, and a few people looked over toward Stacy, who was, of course, pretending to be busy writing something in her notebook. David Kingston was blushing again.

"So," said Ms. Nelson. "I think we deserve to throw ourselves a party to celebrate our success. How does Friday after school sound?"

There were a few cheers from the class.

"But first," she went on, "let's hear how you all made out. Any volunteers?"

Sam Wells raised his hand.

"I thought this project was pretty okay," he said, grinning. "It was really easy, and I had a lot of fun."

Sabrina's hand shot up. "Don't believe a word he says!" she said. "Sure, it was easy for him, and he had a lot of fun. You should have seen how he was acting. He kept tossing the egg around and forgetting to pick it up and stuff. I had to watch out for him all the time!"

Sam turned to her. "Well, it's no wonder you didn't have any fun, Sabrina. You were so serious about the whole thing," he shot back.

Ms. Nelson smiled. "What we have here are two very different approaches to parenting," she said. "Now, Sam is probably the kind of person who would always be ready to play with his child. He might really enjoy taking his son or daughter to an amusement park, and he might not think twice about letting his child ride a unicycle."

"Definitely!" said Sam, grinning.

I noticed that Sabs looked a little hurt. She had been so excited about having a New York model for a teacher and now Ms. Nelson was taking Sam's side.

Ms. Nelson went on. "Sabrina, on the other hand, is slightly more cautious," she said.

"Well, I would never toss a baby across the room, if that's what you mean!" Sabs said hotly, and everyone laughed. "You need to have both kinds of parents to raise a child," said Ms. Nelson. "While Sam would gladly let his child ride an elephant at the zoo, he might forget to feed it unless Sabrina was around to remind him. And it would probably be Sabrina who saw that the child went to the doctor regularly."

Sabs smiled. I could tell that she still liked Ms. Nelson.

Katie raised her hand. "I kind of had the opposite problem with my partner," she said.

Winslow looked at her in surprise, and his glasses slid an inch or so down his nose.

"Katie! What do you mean you had a problem with me?" he asked, amazed. "I was the one who drew up all the charts, who made up all the lists. I was an exceedingly conscientious and responsible partner!"

Katie looked at him sheepishly. "Sorry, Winslow," she said, "but that was kind of the problem. You see, you were so sure about how you wanted to do things, you never even gave me a chance to help out at all."

"Well, if I had needed your help, I certainly would have asked," Winslow replied, pushing his glasses back up on his nose.

"I guess what Katie's trying to tell you is that, to her, parenting is a shared responsibility," said Ms. Nelson. "At least it is in many cases, but not in all cases." She looked at Allison. "Speaking of which, how did our single mother fare?"

Al cleared her throat. "Well," she began. "Actually, at first, I didn't think it was going to be very difficult. I was pretty sure I could handle it on my own. But after a while, I started to wish that there was someone else to share the responsibility with.

"That's why I made this pouch to carry it

in," she continued, holding it out for everyone to see. "I couldn't leave the egg alone, and there was nobody to hand it to when I needed both hands to do something. One time my little brother almost stepped on it. I just managed to save it, and I was so relieved. But there was no one else to be happy about it with, no one else who cared about the egg besides me."

"So, being a single parent wasn't as easy as you thought it might be?" asked Ms. Nelson.

Allison nodded. "It was lonely," she told her.

"What about the rest of you?" she asked. "Did anyone else find that parenting was harder than they expected?"

Quite a few hands went up, including mine.

"Okay, Randy, why don't you tell us about it?" said Ms. Nelson.

I took a deep breath. I had definitely learned a lot of stuff, but I didn't know where to begin.

"Well, first of all, it's definitely easier to be a parent if both partners get along," I started. "But it's not impossible to do it by yourself, either."

I glanced at Mark, who was looking down at his desk. "I know, because my mother basically takes care of me by herself, now that my parents are divorced," I said. "My father lives back in New York, so I don't get to see a whole lot of him." Ms. Nelson nodded. "How do you feel about that?" she asked.

"Well," I said, "at first, I was really mad about it. I hated that my parents were getting divorced, and I would have done anything to stop them. Most of the time I felt like I was ready to explode or something."

Suddenly I realized that the room had grown very quiet. Everybody was listening to me, and I really wanted to stop talking.

But then I looked at Mark. He had turned around in his chair and was staring right at me. I took one more deep breath and went on.

"At first it can be really hard," I said. "Divorce really changes your whole life. You feel like your parents wouldn't be doing this if they really cared about you. So you spend a lot of time wishing things could go back to the way they were, and missing the people and places and things you used to have. But sometimes splitting up can be a good thing for your parents if they're really not getting along. And gradually you get used to it, and eventually you start to have some pretty good new people and places and things in your life."

I looked around. Al, Katie, and Sabs smiled at me. I grinned.

"Well, Randy," Ms. Nelson said, "it sounds to me like you've learned quite a bit from our parenting exercise."

"So have I," Mark whispered, looking right at me. "Thanks."

Chapter Ten

Randy calls Allison.

CHARLIE: (Singing) Raindrops on roses and whiskers on kittens.

RANDY: (Laughing) Are those are a few of your favorite things, Charlie? Hey, let me talk to your sister, okay?

ALLISON: (Picking up the phone) Hello?

RANDY: (Still laughing) Hi, Al, it's me. Listen, I just had an awesome idea.

ALLISON: What?

RANDY: Remember how Ms. Nelson said we should have a party to celebrate the end of the egg project on Friday after school?

ALLISON: Yes.

RANDY: Well, I was thinking that maybe I

should have the party here, at my house.

ALLISON: That's a great idea, Randy. It'll be much more fun at your place than it would be at school.

RANDY: That's what I thought. Anyway, I asked my mother, and she said it was fine with her as long as she didn't have to do any cooking or anything. I'm sure that we can take care of everything, right?

ALLISON: (Thinking) Hmmm . . . We could divide up into groups to make things more organized. How about this? Sabs and I can do the refreshments, and you and Katie can do the decorations and music.

RANDY: Sounds great, Al. Listen, I'll call Katie, and you call Sabs, okay?

ALLISON: Okay. Talk to you soon, Randy.

RANDY: *Ciao!*

Randy calls Katie.

KATIE: Hello?

RANDY: Finally! Katie, I've been trying to

get through to you forever. The phone's been busy.

KATIE: (Sighing) I know, it's Emily. She's been on the phone with her boyfriend!

RANDY: Well, anyway, check this out. I'm going to have the egg project party at my house.

KATIE: Really? Wow! That's great, Randy!

RANDY: Yes. I've already talked to Al, and she and Sabs are going to handle refreshments. Will you handle the decorations and music with me?

KATIE: Sure! Hey, I have a fantastic idea for decorations! Last spring my mom had this big Easter brunch for all my aunts and uncles and cousins. And I bet she's still got some of the decorations around. I could look through them.

RANDY: Well, thanks, anyway, Katie, but I don't think we really want to decorate with a bunch of rabbit stuff.

KATIE: Well, we don't have to use the stuff with rabbits on it, but we could use all the decorations with eggs on them.

RANDY: Oh, right. Sounds cool to me. I'll try to come up with some other ideas, too. Well, I'd better get going.

KATIE: Hey, Randy, can I ask you something?

RANDY: Shoot.

KATIE: Did you really mean it in school today when you said that when your parents first split up you sometimes felt like you were going to explode?

RANDY: Listen, if I start talking about that now, we'll never get this party on the way!

KATIE: Okay, never mind. I guess I'm going to have to climb up into that creepy attic and look for that Easter stuff! Yuck!

RANDY: (Laughing) *Ciao!*

Allison calls Sabrina.

MRS.
WELLS: Hello?

ALLISON: Hello, this is Allison Cloud call-
              ing. May I please speak to
              Sabrina?

MRS.
WELLS: Why, certainly, Allison, dear. Just
              a moment. (Calling) Sabrina! It's
              Allison for you on the phone!

SABRINA: Hi, Allison, what's up?

ALLISON: Hi, Sabrina, I'm calling to tell you
              that Randy has decided to have
              the egg party at her house.

SABRINA: Wow, that's terrific!

ALLISON: And you and I are in charge of
              the refreshments.

SABRINA: How cool! Oh, no, but wait!

ALLISON: What's wrong?

SABRINA: Well, it's just that we're going to
              have to make sure we don't serve
              anything with eggs in it!

ALLISON: Sabs, you're going to have to go

back to eating eggs someday.

SABRINA: Oh, but how can I? After two weeks with that egg, the idea of an egg salad sandwich makes me feel absolutely sick!

ALLISON: Well, I have an idea. Let's think of something that has eggs in it that no one can resist.

SABRINA: Like what?

ALLISON: How about a cake?

SABRINA: That's a great idea! Listen, why don't you come over here, and we can bake it together. Maybe we can even try to make it in the shape of an egg, and use white frosting. But we should probably write something on it. Something like "Congratulations on the Egg Project."

ALLISON: (Laughing a little) How about: "Congratulations on an EGGS-CELLENT JOB!"

SABRINA: Right! See ya later.

Chapter Eleven

"There!" said Katie, climbing down off a ladder and standing back to survey her work. She had just finished hanging a big crepe-paper foldout Easter egg decoration from the center beam of my living room area.

The four of us had run straight to my house after school to get things set up before Ms. Nelson and the rest of the kids got there. I had to admit, the place looked great. Katie and I hung white balloons from all the rafters, and there were collage posters of both human and animal parents and their offspring taped up all over the walls.

Sabrina had come up with this idea that we should all dress in white, in honor of the eggs. It hadn't been easy for me to find an all-white outfit, since so many of my clothes are black. But I had finally settled on a baggy white shirt that used to belong to my father, a white captain's hat I had gotten in an army-navy surplus store in New York, my white long-underwear bottoms, and a pair of bright yellow high-top sneakers. I figured that the yellow could stand for the yolk.

Katie had on a white turtleneck, white jeans, and a white ribbon in her hair. Sabs wore her white sweatshirt, a white gathered miniskirt, white tights, and white flats. She tucked her hair up into a white painter's cap, because she said that red hair absolutely ruined the theme, but the hat kept falling off. Allison was wearing this really nice white turtleneck sweater dress. It looked really great with her long black hair.

Al and Sabs were just finishing setting up their egg-shaped cake on the dining table next to a big bowl of bright pink punch. I guess maybe it was too hard to try to make white punch.

"Well, we're all set!" said Sabrina, sitting down on a chair with a sigh.

"Now all we need are the guests," added Katie.

"That's right," I said. "I can't believe our whole health class is on their way to my house right now."

"Everyone except for four people, that is," Sabrina pointed out.

"Yeah," said Al with a smile. "That was quite a coincidence that Stacy, Eva, B.Z., and Laurel all had dentist appointments at the same time, wasn't it?"

I laughed. I hadn't even wanted to invite Stacy to the party, but Al had convinced me that I had to, since it was supposed to be a class celebration. But I should have known that Stacy wouldn't want to come to a celebration where she couldn't be the star. And, since none of her pals ever did anything without her approval, they had all come up with the same dumb excuse to Ms. Nelson.

Just then, my mother walked in from her studio area. She had been working on her latest plaster sculpture, and her face and hair were covered with the white dust. She had on her "work clothes," an old pair of gray corduroy pants with drips of paint all over them, and a faded plaid flannel shirt. For a minute I felt a little embarrassed, and I wondered if maybe I should ask her to change for the party.

She looked around the living area and smiled.

"Oh, the place looks wonderful!" she said with a sigh.

I grinned. That's one of the nice things about my mother. She can appreciate a bunch of Easter decorations in the middle of the winter. I decided not to say anything about her clothes. It was just too bad if Ms. Nelson and the rest of the class didn't understand.

Then my mother suddenly seemed to notice Al, Katie, and Sabs. As I said, she can be a little spacey when she's working on a project.

"Oh, hi, gang," she said cheerfully.

I waited. This is the moment that always makes Katie and Al feel a little awkward. My mother has told my friends that they can call her by her first name, but no one ever seems to be able to handle it besides Sabs.

Sure enough, Sabrina piped up with "Hi, Olivia!"

"Um, hi," mumbled Katie.

But the big surprise was Al. Instead of her usual quiet "Hello, Mrs. Zak," Al came out with a bold "Hello, Olivia."

I turned to look at her in surprise, but she didn't say anything, just smiled and shrugged her shoulders a little. Sometimes I think Al might be changing in little ways since she's been friends with Katie, Sabs, and me. But I've probably been changing, too, since I've been friends with all of them.

Just then there were voices in the driveway and a knock on the door.

"I hope you don't mind if I just go on working," said my mother, heading back toward her studio area. "I'm in the middle of a crucial part."

As I ran toward the door, I suddenly realized that I was nervous. I think for the first time I realized what I was doing. No one from Acorn Falls had ever been inside my house before — no one except for Al, Sabrina, and Katie, that is. I was pretty sure that no one else at Bradley lived in a converted barn with a single mother who ran around with plaster dust all over her. I took a deep breath and opened the door.

Ms. Nelson was the first one in. Close behind her were Mark, Sam, Mike Epson, Cheryl, David, Winslow, and the rest of the kids. But the biggest surprise was B. Z. Latimer, who came in behind everyone else.

"Hey," I exclaimed as she stepped inside. "I

thought you couldn't come."

She smiled sort of sheepishly. "Listen, Randy, don't tell Stacy, okay? It's just that I really wanted to come. I liked the egg project, and I didn't want to miss the party."

I stared at her. I had always assumed that all of Stacy's friends were just like her, but I guess I was wrong. B.Z. might actually be okay, after all.

"Sure," I managed to say. "Come on in." Just then, Mark walked up to me. He was smiling again, and I decided it definitely looked a lot better on him than that scowl.

"I really like this place," he said, looking around.

"Yeah, me too," I told him. Living in the barn was one of the best parts about being in Acorn Falls. I still thought about my old room in New York once in a while, but our barn had a lot more character, somehow.

"Want me to give you a tour?" I asked him. He nodded.

I led him through the kitchen, past my mother's studio area, back through our living area, and up the stairs to my sleeping loft.

He looked around, amazed.

"This is your room?" he asked me. His blue eyes seemed almost like they were dancing.

I nodded.

"Wow," he said, noticing my drum set in the corner. "Do you play?"

"Yeah," I said.

"We should play together sometime."

I looked at him. "Mark, we don't exactly play the same kind of music," I pointed out.

He grinned. "Well, maybe you could teach me some of your kind of music, and I could teach you some of mine," he said. "Oh, that reminds me." He reached into his back pocket and pulled out a cassette tape. "Here," he said, handing it to me. "This is for you."

I took the tape from him and turned it over in my hand. "Mozart's *Jupiter Symphony*," I read. "Thanks."

"I really like your room," he said. "It seems so . . . you."

"Yeah," I told him, "I guess you're right. It took me a long time to get it look just right. My old room in New York was a lot bigger, and it had a great view."

"How long have you lived here?"

"Just since June," I told him.

He sighed. "Well, I guess maybe I'll get used to my new room after a few months, too," he said.

"You moved?"

"Yeah," he said. "Just last week." His cheeks got a little red. "That's why I couldn't take the egg home with me that day. My mom and I were moving to our new house. You see, my father's a doctor, and he has his office in part of our old house, so when he and my mom split up, she and I moved to a smaller place. She says she likes it better, but I don't know. Sometimes I feel like I'll never get used to it."

"I know what you mean," I said. "It's hard enough having your parents split up. Then you have to go and move on top of it. Hey, at least you don't have to change schools or anything. What's your new room like?"

"Well, we haven't even really finished unpacking, but it's pretty small. It's much smaller than my old room. All my furniture doesn't even fit. I had to leave one of my big old dressers behind. I don't know where I'm going to put all my clothes and stuff."

"Hey," I said suddenly. "You should look at these."

I reached under my bed and pulled out a couple of big white plastic tubs that I use to hold all of my sweaters and T-shirts. They were the same kind of tub that my mother used to mix her plaster in.

"Wow!" he said. "Where'd you get those?"

"My mother ordered them from an artists' supply store in New York," I told him. "But she probably still has the catalogue. I could lend it to you if you want."

He looked at me and smiled. "Thanks, Randy," he said. I got the feeling he was thanking me for more than just the catalogue.

Just then, we heard Sabs calling from downstairs.

"Come on, everyone! We're going to cut the cake!"

"Hey, Mark," I said, "can I ask you a question?"

"Sure."

"Well, you don't have to tell me if you don't want to, but I've been wondering about it for two weeks," I said. "What did you do to get detention that day?"

"Oh," he said, his eyes growing darker for a moment, "I kind of wrote on a desk. I didn't even realize I was doing it at the time. The night before, my mom had told me that we were moving and that she and my dad were definitely splitting up. I was so mad. And I had no one to talk to. I was sitting in social studies, and I wasn't paying attention at all. It was like my head was inside a giant bubble, and I couldn't hear anything that Mr. Grey was saying. The next thing I knew, he was standing over me, and I had carved this big gouge in the desk with my pen."

"I know how that is," I told him. "When my mom first told me we were moving to Acorn Falls, I was really upset. I stormed off to my room and just started throwing my things around. Somehow, I cracked the full-length mirror on my closet door. I don't even know what it was I threw at it."

Mark grinned. "Uh-oh," he said, "seven years of bad luck in Acorn Falls!"

"That's how I felt back then," I told him. "Now I'm not so sure."

We headed down to join the group of kids around the table.

"Where's Ms. Nelson?" I asked.

"Yeah," said Sam. "Ms. Nelson should make

a speech!"

"There she is," said Katie, pointing toward my mother's studio area.

I looked over and saw Ms. Nelson standing near my mother's sculpture, a plastic cup of pink punch in one hand. With her other hand, she was pointing to different parts of the sculpture. My mother, who also had a glass of punch, was nodding, and they seemed deep in conversation.

"Forget it," I said. "Let's leave her alone."

"Cut the cake!" called Andy Grant.

"I'll cut it," said Sabs, picking up the cake-knife.

"And I'll make the speech!" announced Sam, climbing up onto a chair and clapping his hands for attention. He cleared his throat and raised his voice in an imitation of Ms. Nelson. "First of all, I want to say 'congratul-egg-tions' to everyone for finishing this project."

Everyone in the room groaned.

Sam went on. "I think we all did a truly 'eggs-cellent' job."

He was interrupted by several more moans.

"Hey! Hey!" he cried. "What's the matter? Didn't you like my 'yolk'?"

There was some more moaning and groaning.

Then Sabs, who had just finished cutting the first piece, yelled, "Hey, Sam!"

Sam turned to look at her from his place on the chair.

"Catch!" yelled Sabs, laughing, as she tossed him a piece of cake.

Sam fumbled with the cake for a few moments, finally ending up with white frosting all over the front of his shirt and a smashed piece of cake in his hands.

He looked down at Sabs, wild-eyed, from his chair. "This means war!" he cried, jumping down and heading for the cake on the table.

Luckily, I saw what was coming. As quickly as I could, I picked up the entire cake and headed for the front door.

"Cake fight outside!" I announced, as Al opened the door and I ran out onto the front lawn.

As the crowd of screaming kids followed me out the front door, I thought about how lucky I was to have a mother who sometimes didn't notice everything, and about what a good thing it was to have a front lawn to have a cake fight on.

It was funny, but the longer I stayed in Acorn Falls, the more of a surprise it was turning out to be. I was beginning to wonder if living here might not be so bad after all.

Don't Miss
GIRL TALK #8
STEALING THE SHOW

"Hi, Katie!" I said. "Ohmygosh! Where's my math book? Have you seen my math book?"

"Calm down, Sabs. It's right there," Katie said. "What's got you so excited?"

"Today they announce which play the seventh-grade class will be doing this year. I can't wait to see what it is, " I answered. I grabbed her arm and half dragged her down the hallway toward the music room. "Come on, let's go!"

A sign-up sheet for auditions was hanging on the music room door, and a group of people was standing in front of it. Finally enough people moved out of the way so that I could see what was on the sign-up sheet — *Grease: The Musical*.

"*Grease*! That's awesome!" I cried to Katie. "The lead role is Sandy, and she falls in love with this gorgeous guy, Danny. It's so romantic! They even get to kiss in the last scene!"

I pictured Cameron Booth, the guy most likely to get the male lead, and me together onstage as Danny and Sandy, holding hands and singing to each other. Danny and Sandy . . . Sabrina and Cameron . . . It was meant to be!

LOOK FOR THESE OTHER AWESOME
GIRL TALK BOOKS!

MORE GIRL TALK TITLES TO LOOK FOR

Nonfiction
ASK ALLIE 101 answers to your questions about boys, friends, family, and school!

YOUR PERSONALITY QUIZ Fun, easy quizzes to help you discover the real you!

BOYTALK: HOW TO TALK TO YOUR FAVORITE GUY